IMOGENE'S ANTLERS

IMOGENE'S ANTLERS
By David Small

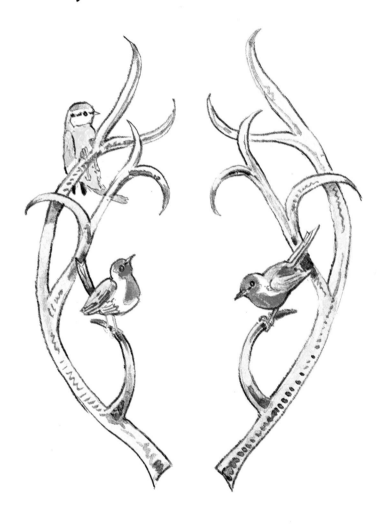

CROWN PUBLISHERS, INC.　NEW YORK

Published by Crown Publishers, Inc.,
225 Park Avenue South, New York, New York 10003.
CROWN is a trademark of Crown Publishers, Inc.
Manufactured in The Netherlands

Library of Congress Cataloging-in-Publication Data
Small, David, 1945-
Imogene's antlers.
Summary: One Thursday Imogene wakes up with a
pair of antlers growing out of her head and causes
a sensation wherever she goes.
1. Children's stories, American. [1. Humourous
stories] I. Title.
PZ7.S638Im   1985   [E]   84-12085
ISBN 0-517-55564-6
ISBN 0-517-56242-1 (pbk)
10   9   8   7   6   5   4   3
First Paperback Edition 1986

To A.B., L.D. and little O.

— D.S.

On Thursday, when Imogene
woke up, she found she
had grown antlers.

Getting dressed was difficult,

and going through a door
now took some thinking.

Imogene started down
for breakfast...

but got
hung up.

"OH!!"
Imogene's mother
fainted away.

The doctor poked, and
prodded, and scratched
his chin.
He could find
nothing wrong.

The school principal
glared at Imogene
but had no advice to
offer.

Her brother, Norman, consulted
the encyclopedia, and then announced
that Imogene had turned into a rare
form of miniature elk!

Imogene's mother fainted again
and was carried upstairs to bed.

Imogene went into the kitchen.
Lucy, the kitchen maid, had her
sit by the oven to dry some towels
"Lovely antlers," said Lucy.

The cook, Mrs. Perkins, gave
Imogene a doughnut, then
decked her out with several more
and sent her into the garden
to feed the birds.

"You'll be lots of fun
to decorate,
come Christmas!"
said Mrs. Perkins.

Later, Imogene wandered upstairs.
She found the whole family
in Mother's bedroom.
"Doughnuts anyone?" she asked.

Her mother said, "Imogene, we have decided there is only one thing to do. We must hide your antlers under a hat!"

Norman telephoned the milliner.

At three o'clock
the milliner
arrived.

Rapidly
he sketched
a few designs,

then set to work.

"Voilà!" said the milliner.

"Bravo! Bravissimo!" cried his assistants.

THUD! Imogene's mother had to be carried away once more.

After dinner,
Imogene practiced
her piano
lesson.

Then, yawning,
she folded her music...

kissed the family...

and went to bed.

Imogene sighed,
remembering the long,
eventful day.

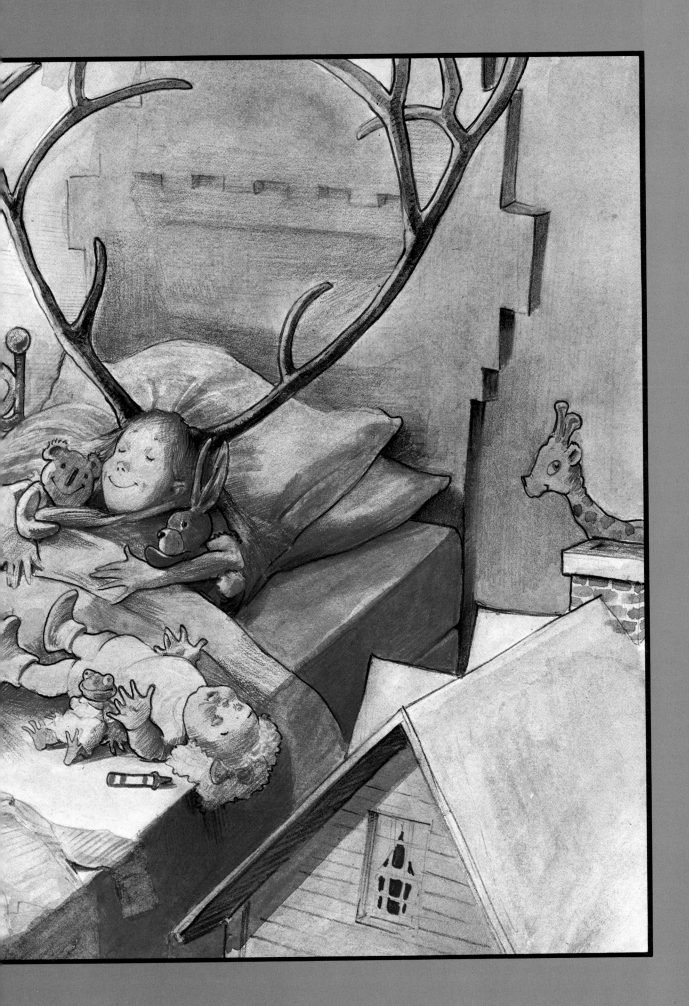

On Friday, when Imogene
woke up, the antlers had disappeared.

When she came down to
breakfast, the family was overjoyed
to see her back to normal…

until she came into the room.

Behind the Scenes

Introduction

In *Imogene's Antlers*, a little girl wakes up one morning wearing a grand pair of antlers and surprises everyone in her family. Overnight, people can grow taller, but as far as we know they can't grow antlers. Even deer don't sprout full antlers overnight.

Animal Ornaments

All male deer grow antlers. But with the reindeer, the female does too. Antlers are made of bone. When they first start to grow, the skin that covers the sprouting antler is called velvet. It even looks and feels like velvet fabric—soft and fuzzy. As they grow, the antlers are very sensitive. The deer carefully avoids striking them on anything hard. As soon as the antlers are fully grown, the velvet dries up and begins to *shed*, or fall off. The deer rubs his antlers against tree trunks and branches to help rub the velvet off. A full set of antlers, or a *rack*, lasts only three months. Once a rack falls off, the whole growing process begins again.

No two sets of antlers are ever exactly alike. The same kind of deer have the same general shape of antler though. The elk has antlers that are broad and flat like great wings over his head. The white-tailed deer has an antler that grows up, then out, then forward, then in. In other words, it's very curvy. At the end of it there are three spikes aiming skyward. The reindeer's antlers form two prongs at the base, each with two or three spikes aimed forward. These different varieties of antlers make every kind of deer a splendid sight in nature.

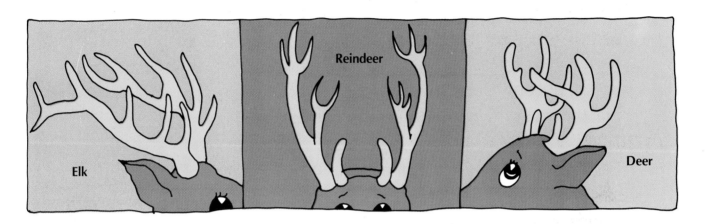

Elk

Reindeer

Deer

Many birds also wear ornaments. For example, the male peacock is famous for his spectacular tail feathers. He carries a train of them behind him sometimes five feet long. When he lifts and opens his tail, it forms a lacy gold, blue and green fan. The fan also has multicolored circles on it called "eyespots." When you see a peacock at the zoo, you'll notice how proudly he carries his feathery ornament. The female, called a peahen, is not so brightly colored.

A bird's head feathers are usually its shortest, but some birds grow long feathers there that form crowns, crests or feather bushes. The cockatoo, a native of Australia and Asia, has a crest that it uses to express itself. When it's excited or frightened or simply trying to impress you, the crest quickly flashes forward.

Behind the Scenes

Odd Features

At very first sight of them, you would say that antlers and peacock tails are pretty special. But nature has also given special parts to many animals that you don't notice right away. These parts are unusual and useful, not only decorative, and they show that the natural world is full of curiosities.

For example, tails are more than simply the end of an animal. The spider monkey's tail is as good as another hand. The spider monkey can grasp things with it. The tail has a tip as sensitive as a finger. This monkey can hang by its tail, use it to hold food, or explore unfamiliar objects from a safe distance with the use of this special tail.

A beaver uses its tail for support. When it is cutting a tree, it stands on its hind legs, so it needs good solid support to hold this position. The beaver's broad, flat tail is just perfect for this job.

The cheetah's long tail maintains balance at top running speed. On a sharp turn, the cheetah holds its tail at a right angle while swinging around. Otherwise, the cheetah would topple over. This is like the long tails of some birds that help both in flight balance and while perching on a branch.

Some tails are used as propellers, to move the animal forward. Alligators never use their legs while swimming. They switch their long thick tails from side to side to swim forward.

Tails can be warning signals, too. A deer's tail, when it droops down, is brown. Upright, it's white. A startled deer immediately raises this white flag to warn other deer, who run away when they see this warning sign. When a skunk raises its tail, it means the skunk is threatening to spray an ugly scent and scare you away. And a rattlesnake gives a warning signal by vibrating the rattle at the tip of its tail.

Behind the Scenes

Tongue in Cheek

Just as your tongue is perfect for licking ice cream cones, some animals' tongues have special uses, too. For instance, a cat's tongue is rough. It is covered with tiny, thorn-like points. When a cat licks itself, its tongue combs away the dirt and cleans its fur.

Dogs use their tongues to cool off when they're hot. They *pant*. Have you wondered why? It's because dogs can't perspire to cool off. The air passing over a dog's tongue and into its throat makes it feel cooler.

You can't stick out your *whole* tongue, but a frog can. Frogs catch crickets, ladybugs and flies with their tongues. When a bug hits a frog's tongue, it sticks, because the tongue is sticky. It's covered with a kind of glue.

A butterfly's tongue is shaped like a straw. It's called a *proboscis* (say: pro-**bahs**-kuss). The butterfly rolls its tongue into a flower to reach the nectar inside. After drinking, the butterfly twirls its tongue up and tucks it under its head until it's thirsty again.

An archerfish lives underwater. If it sees a bug crawling on a plant at water's edge, it shoots it down. How? You guessed it. With its tongue. In the roof of its mouth is a groove. When it presses its tongue to the groove, it forms the bottom of an" O", like a peashooter through which the archerfish shoots "water bullets."

Now You See It, Now You Don't

There are many differences in animals that you can't see. You don't see them because you're not supposed to. The animals are hiding from their enemies. This disguise is called *camouflage* (say: **kam**-uh-flahzh) and it works in several ways.

A baby deer is very helpless and cannot run fast from its enemies. But it can hide from them. Its fur is speckled with white and when a deer stands in the woods, it blends in. The sunlit trees are speckled too, so the deer cannot be seen very easily.

Only a few animals actually change color to match their environment. The snowshoe rabbit is one of them. During summer, the rabbit is grayish-brown to blend into the underbrush and leaves. In winter, white fur grows in to take the place of the summer coat, so the rabbit cannot be seen against the snow. The *chameleon* (say: kuh-**meel**-yon) can change the color of its skin to match its surroundings. If you hear a person called a chameleon, it means that person changes personality from day to day.

Have you heard of animals that play dead? This is another form of camouflage. The opposum is the most well-known of these animals. If cornered or caught, it flops onto the ground and doesn't move. Even its breathing slows. Since most predators prefer live food, they will leave the "dead" opposum. When they do, it runs away. Have you ever heard a person say someone is "playing possum?" What do you think that means?

Odder Than Odd

Some animals are so different they're total oddities. Like the little girl wearing antlers in *Imogene's Antlers*, these animals seem out of place.

When the platypus was first discovered, it was thought to be a joke. It looks part bird, part fish and part animal. It has a bill, webbed feet like a duck, and it lays eggs like a bird but it doesn't have feathers. It has soft, reddish-brown fur. At the tip of its webbed feet it has long claws and has to walk on its knuckles so the claws won't tear the webs.

What would you say if a catfish *walked* by your house one morning? Some folks in Florida recently had that experience. This catfish, originally from Asia, was brought to this country as a tropical pet. But since it has the ability to do a slithery kind of walk, it has escaped from the private ponds and pools where it was put. The walking catfish has walked across many southern states, settling here and there in new pond homes of its own choice.

What passes for a living teddy bear in Australia isn't a bear at all. The *koala* (say: koe-**ah**-lah) is actually a relative of the kangaroo. It sleeps all day and is awake at night in the branches of its home, the *eucalyptus* (say: you-kah-**lip**-tus) tree. Eucalyptus leaves are its only food. It doesn't drink water. It gets all the moisture it needs from the leaves. Though usually quiet, koalas sometimes seem to "argue" with each other in gruff growls. If they are injured, Koalas cry like babies.

Underwater Worlds

The underwater world is as varied and colorful as the one on land. Some fish are long and slender, some short and fat. Some are bright, some are drab. Some catch their food on the surface of the water, others get their food on the bottom. And they come in all sizes — some so tiny we can hardly see them, to some that are larger than we are when they swim near us.

One of the most unusual is the seahorse. It is about six inches long. It has the head of a tiny horse, which is how it got its name. With its head arched, the seahorse swims upright. It has a long tail that it carries in a tight coil or winds around a plant stem. This tail, like the spider monkey's you've already learned about, can grasp things or wrap itself around them.

Another strange creature is the flounder. It is a flat fish that spends most of its time on the ocean bottom. The interesting feature of this fish is that both its eyes are on the same side of its head. At least they are once it's grown up. But at first, a baby flounder swims upright — not flat — and has eyes on either side of its head. When the little fish is one inch long, its right eye starts to move to the left side. The whole change takes place in only four days. The flounder is then able to lie on the bottom and watch for enemies with both eyes.

Most fish stay in the waters they were born in. A fish is suited to certain conditions and has to stay in them to survive. There are natural boundaries to keep them there. The amount of salt in one part of the ocean differs from another. Water temperatures vary a great deal. And water pressure keeps a fish either on the bottom, near the surface or in the middle.

Tropical Reefs

The most spectacular community of fish anywhere is found on the coral reefs of *tropical* oceans. These are warm oceans located around the middle of the globe, between the Tropic of Capricorn and the Tropic of Cancer. A coral reef is made up of millions of tiny creatures called corals. Each coral builds itself a little box of lime to live in. Each box is attached to a neighbor's box. After hundreds of years, a great reef, or sea wall, is built. Different corals are often named for what they look like: there's Elk Coral, Branch Coral, and even Brain Coral.

Brain Coral   Elk Coral   Branch Coral

Since the natural sea wall keeps out the big fish from the open sea, the coral reef is the ideal place for little fish to live. Food is plentiful and enemies few. The little fish of the reefs are among the most unusual and beautiful in the world, and many people enjoy diving in these waters to see them.

One of the most interesting fish on the reef is the butterfly fish. It is bright yellow with black, blue and white markings. It moves in flutters like a butterfly.

Behind the Scenes

The bright blue tang is also known as the surgeon fish. It has a knife-like spine on either side of its body near its tail. It fights off other fish with this sharp spine.

The small needle fish hunts near the surface. It has ridges over its eyes to protect them from the glare of the sun which filters down through the water. It's just like wearing sunglasses all the time!

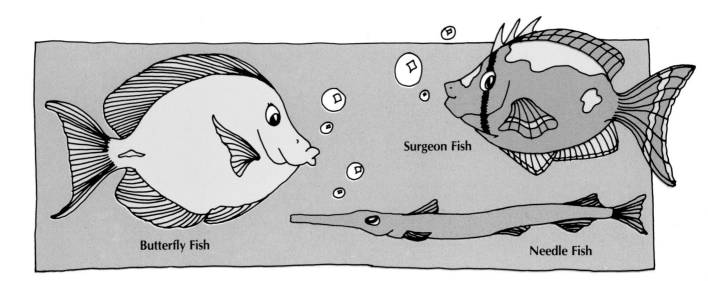

Surgeon Fish

Butterfly Fish

Needle Fish

Bringing The Tropics Home

The best way to learn more about tropical fish is to keep them as pets. But an *aquarium* (say: uh-**kware**-ee-um) means more than a bowl of water with fish in it. The fish need care. They need you to clean their home, feed them and keep them warm. Having an aquarium is work, but the enjoyment of having your own beautiful underwater world is worth every minute.

You need a fish tank that holds at least two quarts of water for each fish, so if you plan to have ten fish, you'll need a twenty quart (or five gallon) tank.

With the tank, you'll need an aerator to put oxygen in the water, and a filter to keep the water clean. You'll also need gravel for the bottom of the tank, and a reflector cover, with or without a light, for the top.

First you set up the tank, adding the water, aerator, filter, gravel and reflector. Let it sit for a few days. Then, add underwater plants, available where you buy your tank. You can get plants that will grow out of the gravel, or you may choose plants that float. A combination of the two types of plants will give you a good underwater garden.

There are hundreds of different kinds of fish, and a trip to your local pet store will give you a good choice. Buy your fish in pairs—a male and female of each kind—so they have company. And you ought to begin with a pair of catfish. Catfish help keep the tank clean by eating the fish food that falls to the bottom of the tank.

Behind the Scenes

Choose your fishy friends by color or size, or just because you like the way they look. Ask your pet store owner if certain fish don't get along, and shouldn't be in the tank together. Ask about feeding instructions, cleaning tips and other fishy things you should know, too. Then, next time Mom or Dad asks if there's something fishy going on, you can say "Yes!" with a big smile.

Our Feathered Friends

Look up to find another world—the world of birds. Like the underwater one, it is filled with surprises and pleasures. There are thousands of different birds, some very odd-looking, some very ordinary. Birds are the most familiar of all wild animals and the easiest to watch. Here are some birds to look for.

BARN OWL

All owls hunt, and they do so at night. Most are brown or gray. They have hooked claws and beaks, and large eyes that look straight ahead. The barn owl lives in barns, steeples, or holes in trees, and can be found across the whole country.

BLUEJAY

This blue and white bird is so noisy it's known almost everywhere. It has a crest and a fan tail. The jay does not have a pretty voice. It can be heard scolding other birds or human intruders. Its favorite food is beechnuts.

CARDINAL

The cardinal is a popular bird on neighborhood lawns. Its bright red feathers, black mask and crest are familiar all over the United States. Its song is a series of loud whistles done rapidly and steadily.

Behind the Scenes

HAWK

There are many kinds of hawks. They all hunt small rodents and birds. When they fly, they alternate wing flapping with long glides. Their short broad wings are for bursts of speed and their long tail balances them on sudden turns. Hawks make a warning "cac-cac-cac" call, so you may hear a hawk before you see one.

RED-WINGED BLACKBIRD

If there are red-winged blackbirds in your neighborhood, you'll know it. In the spring they travel in flocks and sing by the treeful. This blackbird is black with red and orange shoulder stripes.

Animal Riddle

What has the head of a camel, the horns of a deer, the eyes of a rabbit, the ears of a bull, the neck of a snake, the scales of a fish and the claws of an eagle? A dragon, that's what. You've never seen one? That's because the dragon is a mythical creature. A *mythical* creature lives only in the imagination. Yet through the ages people have believed in them, and there are many stories told and written about fierce and friendly dragons alike.

48

If they were to walk the earth, dragons would be very odd indeed. Not only would they look strange, but they'd have nasty tempers, too. Dragons, according to the myths, breathe fire. They live underground in caves and come out only at night. They eat whatever crosses their paths—sheep, cows, or even people—but dragons are thought to prefer swallows. A dragon could be tamed to guard a great treasure if it were fed swallows every day.

Most dragons are afraid of nothing, but some are afraid of eagles and thunder. A man could kill a dragon in a swordfight, but it wouldn't be easy. A story is told of a German dragon that could be conquered by a tickle under its chin, but many men were eaten before one got close enough for that fatal tickle.

Parts of dragons have been used in magic. If you were to drink dragon's blood, you might have the power to talk to birds. And a dragon's heart buried at your doorstep would keep the house safe and bring good luck. Dried dragon's eyes mixed with honey, it is said, cure nightmares. And, no doubt, give a few too.

All in all, there are more stories told about the dragons of myth than there are about most real creatures. Why don't you make up a dragon? Get out a piece of paper and some crayons, and make a dragon portrait. Then, why not make up a story about your very own dragon?

Behind the Scenes

"Little Brother Of The Arctic"

During winter storms, the north Atlantic ocean is a place of icy winds and huge waves. Yet there is a remarkable bird that makes its home by this ocean on the coast of Newfoundland. This bird is the puffin, one of the most unusual and toughest of animals.

The puffin is very striking to look at. Like a small penguin, it stands upright and waddles when it walks. Its cheeks are puffy. It has a big, horny orange beak with dark blue plates above the eyes that give it a worried look. Dark lines of feathers run back from the eyes, looking somewhat like teardrops. At certain times each year, the beak changes color, becoming striped with red, blue-gray and ivory.

A puffin's wings are short and powerful. It flies close to the surface of the ocean in even the strongest winds, sometimes dipping under the waves and using its wings as paddles. The puffin's eyelids are *transparent*. This means it can see through them. If a puffin closes its eyes underwater, it can still see. The puffin has a thick layer of fat on its body to protect it from the freezing cold water.

Puffins are usually quiet birds. Sometimes, however, they make interesting sounds. They purr and croak during friendly squabbles. And one of their calls sounds a lot like a chain saw. Eskimos call the puffin the "little brother of the Arctic."

Activities ➡

A Letter Game

How many words can you make with the letters that spell antlers? Use the letters in the circle. For starters, find the words ANT, SEAL and STAR.

Score yourself:

8 words   =   Great
12 words =   Terrific
15 words =   Fantastic

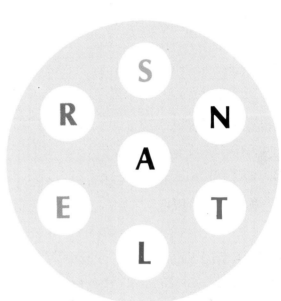

A Feather Pen

Long ago people made pens out of large feathers. You can make a modern feather pen. Find a large feather in the yard or the park. Get a plastic straw. Stick the feather in one end of the straw. Slip a pencil in the other end. That's all there is to do. Why not make another one for a friend!

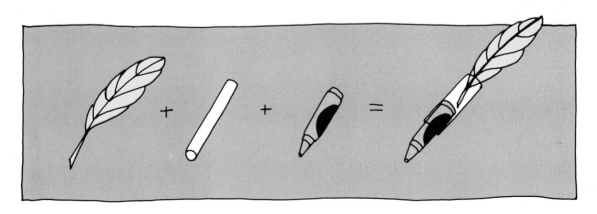

Activities

Feed Your Friends

Treat the birds to a special meal. You'll have as many birds in your yard as Imogene did.

What You Need:

peanut butter   large pine cones
bird seed   string

What You Do:

1. Mix the peanut butter and bird seed.
2. Stuff the mixture between the petals of a pine cone.
3. Use a piece of string to make a hanger for the cone. Loop the string under some petals near the top.
4. Make several cones and hang them outside your window or from the branch of a tree.

Trivia Game

Trivia are facts that may be unimportant but are very interesting. You can make up a game using trivia. Here are some to start you off. Put them on cards. Write the question on one side and the answer on the other. Stump your friends.

1. Q. Which is the largest zoo, the San Diego Zoo (California) or the Bronx Zoo (New York)?
   A. The San Diego Zoo is home to the largest number of zoo animals in the world.

2. Q. Where was the first Morgan horse *foaled* (born), in New York or Massachusetts?
   A. "Justin Morgan" was the first of the breed of Morgan horses. He was foaled in 1793 in Massachusetts.

3. Q. Which is larger, an African elephant or an Asian elephant?
   A. African elephants are larger and have enormous floppy ears.

Picture Puzzles

Each puzzle names a bird that Imogene saw in her yard. Guess each name. Here's how to solve the puzzles. First, write the name of each picture on a piece of paper. Also, copy the extra letters and the signs, too. Now you can follow the signs to add or subtract the letters. We've done one for you. Can you figure out the other two?

– IDER + ⬤ – MBLE + ➡ – AR =

S P A R R O W

+ 🏚 – CAB + ⬤ – BL = _ _ _ _ _ _ _

– OT + 👑 – KG = _ _ _ _ _ _

Activities

Hat Factory

Hats are worn in many kinds of jobs.
Can you match the hat to the job?

fire hat
police officer's hat
football helmet
chef's hat
top hat
cowboy's 10-gal. hat
clown's hat

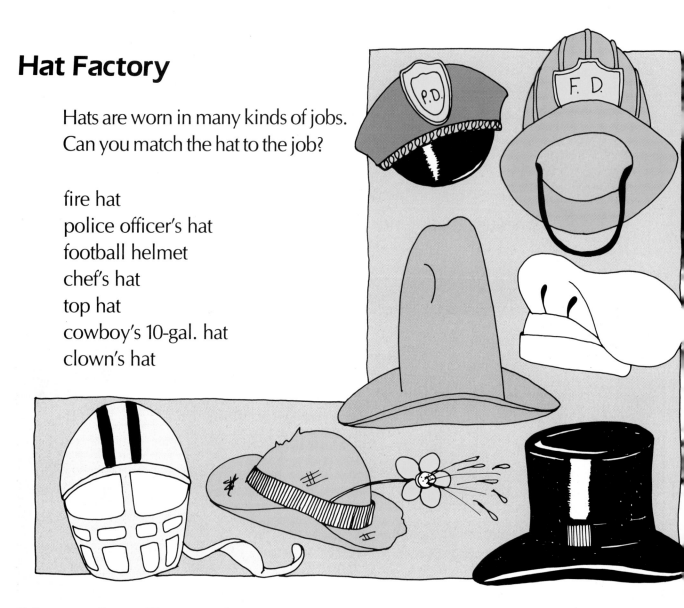

Name It—Draw It

Put your imagination into high gear for this activity. Look at the three lists on page 55. Choose a kind of shop, a name and an address. The name and address should give a clue to what the shop sells. On another piece of paper, draw an advertisement for your shop, like the yellow pages ad we've done for Big Bucks Bank.

A	B	C
Kind of Shop	*Name of Shop*	*Address*
Bakery	Spokes	Boot Hill
Bank	Heels	Wheeler Rd.
Bike Shop	Baits	Cooks Rd.
Fish Fry	Big Bucks	Pier Point
Hat Shop	Sweets	High St.
Shoe Shop	Bonnets	Gold St.

Did You Know…?

On the other side of the world, in China, most people use fans. The women prefer round fans and the men prefer folding fans.

The yo-yo that you and your friends like to play with was first used by children in China many hundreds of years ago.

The giant panda that comes from China is called a bear but it really isn't a bear. The panda is a member of the raccoon family.

Activities

Pretty As A Peacock

Take another look at Imogene with peacock feathers. What a pretty picture! Make your own peacock fan. Just follow these easy steps.

What You Need:
a flat paper plate
a Popsicle stick
glue or tape
crayons

What You Do:
1. Use the picture at right as a model.
2. First draw the body of the peacock in the center of the plate.
3. Color in all the blue and green feathers.
4. Glue or tape the Popsicle stick to the back of the plate.
5. Keep the fan handy for a hot day.

Word Search

Hidden in the maze below are words you've just learned. Do you remember what they mean? The words go across and down. Find the words in the maze and then write them on another paper.

BREAKFAST, TOWELS, HAT, MINIATURE, POKED, PRINCIPAL, MOTHER, CHIN, ELK, ANTLERS, KISSED, FAINTED, SCRATCHED

Q	B	R	E	A	K	F	A	S	T
M	V	X	L	N	I	A	Z	C	M
O	W	Z	K	T	S	I	R	R	P
T	O	W	E	L	S	N	H	A	T
H	B	Q	X	E	E	T	W	T	V
E	C	L	U	R	D	E	X	C	Z
R	H	Z	V	S	L	D	B	H	F
M	I	N	I	A	T	U	R	E	Z
F	N	X	Q	P	O	K	E	D	P
X	P	R	I	N	C	I	P	A	L

Activities

Hide And Seek

These kids are having a picnic lunch. But there are five uninvited guests: an ant, a spider, a toad, a grasshopper and a squirrel. Can you find them?

Pitch A Tent

Make a stay-at-home jungle tent. Just cover a folding table with a sheet and you have a tent. You might use two chairs instead of a table. Place the chairs back-to-back. Leave space between the chairs for yourself and a friend. Now you have a special place to tell stories. Think about all the animals named in this book and make up lots of jungle adventures.

A Surprising Day

In *Imogene's Antlers*, Imogene woke up one day to find that she'd changed. What would you do if you woke up one day and you were ten feet tall? You can choose your own ending. Just pick what you would do each time the story stops.

A. You wake up and your legs are hanging over the end of the bed. You jump up and hit the ceiling. Do you...
   - Smile, laugh and call your Mom and Dad (*go to B*)
   - Cry and try to hide. There is no where you can fit (*go to D*)

B. When your folks see you they holler "Hooray!" You all jump for joy. Do you...
   - Call the coach of a basketball team (*go to C*)
   - Send a telegram to the circus manager (*go to E*)

C. The basketball coach comes to visit. He will hire you for a million dollars. But you must leave home for five years. Do you...
   - Tell him you get dizzy after you run a long time (*go to F*)
   - Ask him if you can play for only one year (*go to E*)

D. Go back to sleep for a day. You may return to normal tomorrow.

E. You are told you aren't needed. Try another time.

F. You can overcome your problems. Be brave and have fun.

Activities

When you want to know what a word means, you go to a dictionary or a word book. Bet you won't find these words and meanings in your dictionary!

CARTOON	a song you sing in an automobile
HANDSOME	a word you use when you want something passed to you
LIPSTICK	what you wear when you want to keep your mouth shut
VITAMIN	what you do when someone comes to your door
X-RAY	belly vision

It's spelling time....

Can you spell mousetrap with three letters?   C - A - T

What seven letters did Mother Hubbard say when she went to the cupboard?   O - I - C - U - R - M - T

Tulip Garden

Look at the tulip garden on the next page. These bees have been collecting nectar in the garden all day. Tip toe through the tulips without bothering a busy bee. Start at the ENTRANCE and find your way through the garden with your finger. If you come face to face with a buzzing bee, turn back. Find another path to the garden EXIT.

ENTRANCE

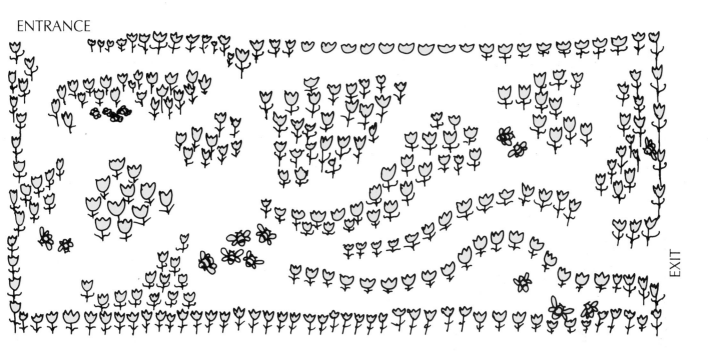

EXIT

Looking Back

How good are you at finding details in a story? Hunt through *Imogene's Antlers* to find the answers to the questions below.

1. On what day did Imogene wake up with antlers?
2. How many birds perched on Imogene's antlers?
3. What musical instrument did Imogene play?
4. How many times did Imogene's mother faint?
5. In what month did this story take place?
6. How many lollipops did the doctor have?
7. How many men in the story had mustaches?
8. What was the kitchen maid's name?
9. What time did the clock show?
10. How many times did the cat appear?
11. What did Imogene's mother wear around her neck?
12. How many pictures hung on Imogene's bedroom wall?

1. Thursday 2. 8 3. piano 4. 3 5. May 6. 3 7. 3 8. Lucy 9. 1:15 10. 13 11. beads 12. 2

Activities

Animal Library

If animals could read, what books would they like? An octopus might read *Eight Ways To Shake Hands*. Look at each book title. It is a clue to an animal. Match the animals to the book titles below.

Hop To It

Big Cheese Meets Little Cheese

Be My Honey

Mystery In The Old Trunk

Cooking In A Sty

Roaring River

Home Tweet Home

Cloud Gazing

Clouds often form pictures in the sky. What do you see in these clouds? Read the clues if you need a hint.

Clues

- I live in the ocean deep.
- Little Bo Peep lost me.
- I was home to a Native American.
- I am king of the jungle.

Activities

Mirror Image

Here is a message from someone who wishes to keep her name a secret—except to those friends who can unravel this mysterious letter. Do you think it's written in a foreign language? Or maybe it's just a funny message in gobble-dee-gook?

DEAR FRIENDS,
COME TO MY PARTY AND HELP ME CELEBRATE MY BIRTHDAY.

PLACE: NEW YORK HARBOR
DATE: JULY 4TH
SEE YOU THERE!
THE STATUE OF LIBERTY

Have you figured it out? Well, we'll give you a hint on how to *decipher* (say: dee-**sigh**-fur), or figure out, the code. All you have to do is hold this page up to a mirror to read it.

You may want to use this code with your friends. You can send your own secret messages, or you, too, can use it for party invitations.

Here is a chart to help you out.

I	H	G	F	E	D	C	B	A
R	Q	P	O	N	M	L	K	J
	Z	Y	X	W	V	U	T	S
9	8	7	6	5	4	3	2	1

As you can see, the letters of the alphabet and the numbers are printed backwards. Remember that the words on each line of your note must also be printed backwards. Practice your mirror writing letter by letter. Then, you'll be ready to write secret messages in code!